hops   c
se

MONSTER BOOKS

Henley-on-Thames . MMXXI

BUK

Robin Bennett

Buk (Aktuel Translations Ltd. T/A Monster Books)

Published in Great Britain in June 2021 by
   Monster Books
   The Old Smithy
   Henley-on-Thames
   Oxon. RG9 2AR

First published 2021.

ISBN 978-1-9163751-54

A catalogue record of this book is available
from the British Library.

Printed by Clays Ltd., Bungay.

If you love what you have,
the world belongs to you

In the beginning was the Word ...
meaning sound and narrative.

The Earth was all scorching heat,
with melted rock and twisting skyscrapers
of flame and noise.

Then the sounds became the gentle winds
that cooled the infernos, fused the rock
and condensed the seas. Animals and then
people came, and the narrative multiplied
as millions of tales were spun and the
Earth revolved.

Buk, who had been there from the very
start, read the stories and he laughed
with pure delight.

Chapter 1

I n nearly every old town up and down the country, tucked away in a quiet street, you'll find a worn stone.

Usually it just sits there – poking out of the pavement or half-covered by the side of a building – worn, a bit grubby and ignored.

Nancy, who often went to town on shopping trips with her parents, used to wonder what they were there for.

Or at least she did until the day she met Buk ...

It was early June. To Nancy, who was walking down Bell Street in Henley-on-Thames (keeping her usual three feet behind her mother) it felt more like August. In Cairo.

The sun had blazed down throughout May and although it was technically still spring in England, the grass had already turned brown in the middle of their lawn and the pavements in town were hot and unpleasantly sticky. Little black bubbles of tar seeped up through the cracks and Nancy was concentrating so hard on squishing them back down that she didn't immediately notice the strange boy watching her from across the street. When she did, she actually glanced up at a shop window on her right, so what she saw was really only his reflection on her side of the street.

There was something oddly interesting about him: his clothes were dusty and had a homemade look and he looked extraordinarily still – and calm – amidst a world on the move. But mostly her attention was caught by the fact that he was sitting on one of those odd little stones she had always seen in town. She gazed at his reflection for a few moments, noticing that he was also barefoot. He appeared to be smiling, very directly, at her, so she turned her head in order to give him her *hard look*.

However, when she looked across the street, the stone was empty.

The really curious thing, though, was that when she turned back to the reflection in the shop window, she was startled to see him still there. He was reading something now, a sort of sheet, like a parchment – a curtain of almost-white hair falling across his eyes.

He glanced up and gave Nancy a shy wave, before a bus went past, obscuring her view.

By the time it had moved on he was no longer there. She even checked the shop window reflection, just to be sure.

'My back's killing me.' Her mum looked hot and a bit cross. As usual.

Nancy suddenly realised that she was also lugging a heavy plastic carrier bag full of milk and fruit. She moved up level with her mum and took hold of the bag. 'I can carry these to the car,' she said but her mother just pursed her lips and tightened her grip on the bag as she crossed the road.

Nancy caught up.

'How's the Molehill?' she asked, feeling the swish of the plastic bag against her bare legs. It was her Dad's name for It. Neither he, nor Nancy had quite been able to bring themselves to actually say, *the baby* yet.

Her mother was now rummaging for keys in her handbag. 'I feel like I've got a radiator strapped to my stomach. You know, I never thought I would say this, but I hope the weather takes a turn for the worse. Soon.'

'Me too,' Nancy patted her mother's arm to be companionable and gave what she hoped sounded like a grown-up sigh.

Half an hour later they were back in the kitchen at home. The overhead fan was on full blast and the window open. Her mother was rinsing lettuce for a salad as Nancy perched on the edge of the kitchen table, watching her.

She was congratulating herself over the fact she had been nice to her mum all afternoon, which she hoped went some way to make up for the terrible weekend. There had been at least two quiet, sort of hissy arguments between her parents when they'd had friends around for a barbeque and then a couple of proper shouty ones when they were alone – the last one had made her mum cry. Nancy had been cross with her dad for being horrible to her mum but part of her being cross was she felt guilty – that she sort of agreed with him.

Most of their arguments these days were about the Molehill and the fact that her mum was too old to be having a baby and it was making her ill. She'd overheard her father saying something about high blood pressure. Nancy just didn't get why her mum was so keen to have a baby anyway. She'd had Nancy ages ago and Nancy had assumed – as soon as she was old enough to think about it seriously – that her parents had sort of got the whole baby thing out of their system by now. Otherwise why would they have waited nearly thirteen years to have another one?

At this rate, Nancy was going to feel more like an aunt than a big sister. Secretly she was also terrified her dad would just lose the plot completely one day and leave them before the baby was born: and from that day on, Nancy and her mother would be really poor and she would probably have to miss school and seeing all her friends in order to help look after the Molehill at home, and push It aimlessly around the park and the shops in the wind and the rain.

People might even think it was her baby.

Nancy put that thought firmly back in the imaginary chest that was in her head marked, *Do NOT Touch*. Unfortunately, it was more of a Jack-in-the-Box these days and had a tendency to spring open without warning – spilling its contents straight out of her mouth, via her brain.

Her mum suddenly smiled, looking out of the kitchen window at nothing in particular.

'You remember those stones in town you always used to talk about? The little round ones you find on the corners. They're always sort of worn and round on top ... like someone's been sitting on them for a long time?'

Nancy blew a lick of dark brown hair from her face and looked up sharply. 'Of course,' she said. It was another one of those weird coincidences that seemed to happen rather a lot lately. She could have sworn her mum had suddenly become psychic since she'd got pregnant. And a little psychotic, too.

'You used to ask, "What are they actually for?" and I would say, "I don't think they're actually *for* anything dear – not at least these days. They may have had something to do with marking routes, or distances, or perhaps something to do with horses ... your father might know ... he seems to have an opinion on pretty much everything these days ... ' Her mother broke off abruptly, biting her lip. A cucumber was, at that moment, tasting cold steel in her hands. 'Anyway, I saw one in town today and I thought of what you used to say and then I thought I saw someone on it. Just a shadow, hardly that ... '

Nancy's mouth had fallen open. 'I saw someone sitting on one of them today too, just off Market-place! A boy.'

Her mother smiled. 'Well, then I remembered your imaginary friend when we were on holiday, what was her name? Sad Sue – whatever happened to her?'

Half annoyed at herself and half alarmed, Nancy felt herself blush. She never used to turn into a beetroot at the drop of a hat. 'Her name was *Sue*, just *Sue*, and she was only sad because you left her behind, on the beach in Cornwall. And it was freezing cold.'

But her mother had already switched off. She did that a lot these days – it was as if Nancy wasn't there anymore. Wincing she put her hand on the small of her back. 'It'll be any time soon now … I wish the baby would move off my hip.' And just like that the conversation was forgotten. Her mother polished off the cucumber with a flourish.

A few minutes later, Nancy quietly slipped off upstairs; basically to brood.

Everyone, including her best friends, agreed that Nancy had a habit of retreating into her own fantasy world from time to time. Usually when she was upset about something.

Chapter 2

That night Nancy dreamt she was walking by herself in a wood. The ground upon which she trod was soft and pleasingly springy. She looked down and saw that she was barefoot. In spite of the fact she was wearing just a thin, cotton nightdress, Nancy wasn't the slightest bit cold.

A thick, dark green moss grew along the narrow path she trod, spreading out, the further she walked, all the way to the base of the trees. As she went deeper into the wood, the moss began to grow up their broad trunks until it hung in soft, fleecy blankets from the branches and everything had a fairytale emerald glow about it.

Between the trees, she could make out a pink morning sun rising over the mist. A small, brightly-coloured cottage nestled amongst the trees, emitting a trickle of smoke from a chimneystack that looked like a chocolate roll. Oddly though there was no birdsong and, before long, Nancy began to feel very alone and a little scared.

Then she heard a voice a little way off.

'I found a star,
The Brightest Star,
In the month of May,
And this star, the brightest star,
Said that she would stay.
We sought a star,
The Tiniest Star,
Amongst thousands in the sky,
And this star, the Tiniest Star lies still … so still
in the orbit of mine eye.

And sometimes now,
When I lie awake,
I hear a passing at my door.
And another star, the Wisest Star
whispers, 'Nevermore …
Nevermore …'

The recitation broke off abruptly as Nancy came around the corner and found herself face to face with the boy from Marketplace, sitting on what looked like the very same stone she'd seen that day.

He glanced up from his parchment and smiled, but with his light grey eyes only. 'Wake up sleepy head.'

And so she did.

Nancy lay there feeling excited. It was only now dawning on her why what she'd seen yesterday was so peculiar – that's to say someone who appeared in a reflection only. Fresh from her dream, she also suspected it might be one of those situations where one person (Nancy) was the only one who was able to see the other person (the ash-blond boy).

And Nancy could be surprisingly purposeful when she had a mind to be. Jumping out of bed, she climbed into a pair of old jogging shorts, her new t-shirt and some old but barely used trainers – the better to slip out of the house quietly before anyone else woke up.

Just as she was moving towards the back door, Elgar, their Labrador, came padding across the kitchen, his tail wagging, eyes hopeful. Nancy looked at him for a few moments and then decided that it would be heartless to leave him now he was up and wide awake and anyway, dogs were good cover.

Quite what she needed cover for, she hadn't really thought through but she planned to get to the bottom of the boy on the stone without delay and she already had an inkling that any answers she found weren't likely to be parent-friendly. *I was out walking the dog,* was as good an excuse as any.

She grabbed his lead and opened the back door, as Elgar slipped through her legs and ran to the end of the garden to see if there was anyone worth barking at through a hole in the fence.

Luckily it was too early, even for the postman.

An hour and a half later, she was back at home looking miserably at a breakfast she didn't fancy eating. It had been a let down from high expectations, a complete waste of time and utterly embarrassing. She'd wandered around the centre of town with Elgar trotting along the pavement in front of her, looking at all the stones on the street corners and glancing in the reflections of shop windows.

She went up the street leading to Marketplace four times until eventually she began to feel like a complete idiot.

She was just turning to go, when she felt very faint: so Nancy stopped walking and closed her eyes. Just for a moment, she had the impression she was in quite another place altogether: a vast building of corridors and cold echoes … and she was quite abandoned. Nancy felt a sense of cold panic and raced home through the eerie streets as fast as she could.

Back in the safety of her kitchen, everything was back to feeling normal and she found she could think clearly.

Nancy reached two conclusions: Firstly, she had imagined the whole thing the day before – the boy was no more real than her dream and, secondly, she'd just realised that she'd never really liked cereal.

Chapter 3

Three weeks passed, almost without her being aware. The weather got even hotter (incredibly) and then the summer holidays finally started.

One Friday morning she was in town on her own. This was unusual, as most days during holidays she would meet her best friend, Millie, by the ice cream van in the park that lay just out of town by the river. However, that morning, when she got there she had caught sight of Millie from a distance. Lately, Millie had seemed rather sad about something, but now Nancy saw she was chatting with her creepy new friend, Darren (who Nancy suspected was actually turning into a *proper* boyfriend). And perhaps it was because of this potential-new-*actually*-first-ever-boyfriend situation that she was looking more cheerful than she had done in weeks. On an impulse, Nancy texted to say her mum had asked her to do some shopping at the last minute and so she wouldn't be able to make it.

She'd known Millie since pre-school – she was as blond as Nancy was dark; curly haired and freckled in contrast to Nancy's long straight locks and pale complexion. Plus Millie couldn't stop talking – Nancy had secretly timed her over a period of weeks and her record of silence was a pitiful thirty-eight seconds – she would often chat away for both of them whilst Nancy looked on, viewing the world through a solemn gaze that rarely faltered. People always remarked that they made an *interesting* pair but over the last year Nancy found she had less and less in common with her best friend. Especially when it came to Darren who was nearly fourteen and into black t-shirts, skinny jeans and not brushing his teeth – or washing his hair, apparently.

So, instead of hanging out by the band at the river, where it was relatively cool, Nancy found herself mooching about in the baking centre of town amongst the tourists, the elderly shoppers and traffic fumes.

Near the steps leading to the town hall there was a stall selling cheap summer clothes, straw hats and sunglasses. Since the heat wave began, stallholders around town had jumped on the bandwagon and it looked like everyone was now selling floaty dresses, floppy head gear and those hand-held fans that mysteriously stopped working after a day, if the propeller didn't come off first and hit you in the face.

Nancy was trying (without much success) to get a pair of white-framed sunglasses off a revolving rack, when she spotted *him*.

He was perched on a stone, with his parchment thingy, looking directly at her. Feeling self-conscious, she quickly stopped what she was doing and pretended she hadn't seen him by looking the other way. Unfortunately, the other way was two dogs sniffing each other's bottoms, so she had to turn back quickly. To her alarm, he was now beckoning at her to come over. Nancy made a *who, me?* hand signal and the boy rolled his eyes in a *who else?* gesture.

'That's a good trick,' was all she could think of saying when she got across the square. His eyes were the greyest she'd ever seen, and she couldn't help noticing that his lashes, like his hair, were almost pure white and unusually long and thick.

'What is?' he asked, squinting up at her through them.

'Your disappearing act last time we met.'

'Um, yes, I suppose you're right,' he nodded whilst looking like he hadn't got a clue what she was talking about. The paper he was holding looked incredibly old, the sort of thing you'd see in a museum or a film. The writing itself was intriguing: the script looked familiar but none of the actual letters resembled anything she'd seen before. Even more puzzling, the letters moved on the page – disappearing, reforming and always changing shape. A couple of times, and only for the merest of moments, she thought she saw a word she knew, randomly appearing on the screen – *house … me … time … ergo* … .

'Is that thing electronic?' she asked.

The boy peered at the parchment curiously for a few moments as if he was seriously considering the question. 'I don't think so,' he said.

'Who are you?' Nancy's natural curiosity getting the better of her. Her mother was always telling her off for being rude but, honestly, sometimes she couldn't help it.

Oddly, the boy seemed equally confused by this question as he was the first. 'I'm … er … my name is Buk.'

'What, as in *book* book? That's a nickname, surely?' He shrugged and then went straight back to staring at the continually reforming characters on his device.

When it was obvious that he wasn't going to answer she carried on. 'So, um, what are you doing here?' Nancy gestured – more at the stone than anywhere else.

Buk – if that really was his name – looked relieved at being asked a question he was reasonably sure of answering. 'Oh, *that* ... I'm here to help.'

'Help who?'

'Help you.'

Which she thought was an odd thing to say. Her mum was the only person she knew who needed help.

But she couldn't ask him any more questions because he had suddenly vanished. Like a magic trick.

Again.

Chapter 4

Nancy was totally flabbergasted.

She stood looking at the empty stone for a full thirty seconds before she realised that a dog, whose lead was hooked on a post outside a shop, was barking angrily at the stone – and at her. She moved off, scurrying in confusion down a side alley. The dog looked like it was thinking about trying to follow – lead or not – but evidently decided it was too hot to go chasing strangers about town, so sat down again.

Nancy looked at her hands, which were shaking and wondered what in blue blazes was happening to her. On the face of it, saying things like *blue blazes*, probably meant she was turning into her dad. However, talking to strangers in the street who had a habit of disappearing under your nose was a different matter entirely. There was only one logical explanation. She was losing it. Nancy decided to go home immediately. She needed to ask her mum if there was a history of madness in the family.

However, when she got home, she found that no-one was about.

Nancy's parents had bought a large Victorian house fifteen minutes' walk from the centre of town when Nancy had started school. Her mum loved it because she was a painter, and the upstairs loft had been converted by the previous owners into a large spare room that made the perfect studio. A row of skylights ran down one side of the sloping roof and, at the end, as a kind of finishing touch, was a perfectly round window that looked out onto an old cemetery, some pea-green paddocks and a small copse that shielded the town from the sight of people playing golf on the local golf course.

It was freezing up there, at the top of the house, in the winter and stuffy in the summer but you can't have everything and Nancy's mother didn't seem to notice. Most days, she spent hours in her studio, slapping paint onto gigantic canvases that usually depicted enormous flowers very close up, as if you had been magically shrunk to the size of a bee.

Nancy had heard her mother's pictures sold very well in Japan and she'd once even seen a reproduction of one in a book on art that had been lying around the design room at school.

Her dad was also slightly famous. He conducted an orchestra in Oxford and was always meeting other semi-famous people who sometimes came to the house and either made a great big fuss of Nancy or ignored her completely.

The embarrassing truth of the matter was that they could only just afford to live so close to town in such a large house and *this* meant that money was another issue between her parents these days. Recently her dad had been forced to sell his car – a classic burgundy Alvis with over-stuffed leather seats, like a favourite uncle's armchair. It broke his heart to get rid of it, especially as now he had to cycle or walk to the station in all weathers to catch the train to Oxford or London.

Nancy doubted they were poor but she was pretty sure they weren't as comfortably off as some of her friends whose parents owned attractive ponies and Italian holiday homes and shiny new 4x4's that smelled of wax and shampooed leather, as opposed to one ancient Volvo that usually smelled of oil paints and wet dog.

She told her friends at school that her dad was a conductor. The first time one of her other friends, Lucy, came around to visit she'd stopped in the street outside, staring up at the gothic brickwork and then at the large garden with its towering rhododendrons and rose bushes and remarked that there was obviously more money in collecting bus fares than she'd thought. After that incident, Nancy was careful to be a bit more specific.

In the kitchen, she found a note in her mum's handwriting on the table.

In case you didn't get my text — gone to the hospital — there's a lasagne in the deep freeze. Be back later.

In spite of the casual tone, the note actually made Nancy feel giddy with worry. Her dad probably wouldn't be back for hours. She wondered if she should go to the hospital to keep her mum company, but she hated the place and she also suspected her mum would probably be more cross than grateful that she was there. It had seemed to Nancy that recently she'd taken distant parenting to a whole new level. She never really looked at her when speaking and, when Nancy held her mother's arm –

something she had always done – her mother often flinched, as if touched by something either very hot or very cold.

It would have been easy to blame the baby and the fact she wasn't well, but Nancy couldn't help feeling there was something else.

Either way, she'd just lost her appetite.

Chapter 5

~

What on earth are you wearing?'

Buk looked startled and then a bit embarrassed or possibly just confused, which made Nancy feel mean. Something about him reminded her of how she felt on her first day at school.

'Um, what's wrong with, er, which bit?' he asked, vaguely running a hand down his sleeve.

'Well, you can get away with being barefoot in this heat, and the bright green trousers I imagine could be some kind of statement ... but ski goggles?'

'Oh good,' remarked Buk, looking relieved and pulling them off, 'they keep the sun off but they're actually quite uncomfortable.'

'You don't say.' Nancy yawned unexpectedly. ' – excuse me, I'm just tired,' she said quickly, in case it looked like she was bored. 'My mum didn't get back from the hospital until late last night and I stupidly waited up for her.'

To tell the truth, she had no good excuse for being that tired. After she had read her mother's note, she'd spent most of the rest of the day sitting on her bed, listlessly watching the sun move across the sky, going from yellow to a sort of unearthly dark orange as it dipped below the trees. Then evening had gathered up the stray shadows into one and Nancy had dozed.

Hours later, both her parents came back looking drawn. They hung up their jackets in the hallway in silence, more like two strangers who just happened to arrive at a restaurant at the same time, and her mother had gone straight to the kitchen, leaving her father alone in the hall.

Nancy, sitting on the landing, staring silently through the banisters, had wanted to ask if everything was alright with her mother, but she could see things obviously weren't, and so she got up and tiptoed back to her room.

Later, Nancy had another dream. This time she was racing down a long road. Cars popped up in her field of vision left and right, so she assumed it must be a motorway. As the vehicle she was in accelerated, she felt a brief surge of exhilaration that turned to mild panic as something told her they were going too fast.

She opened her eyes.

The house was quiet as a morgue. Nancy got up, drawn by a light at the window. The cemetery outside had long since stopped worrying her – nevertheless, tonight it looked more sinister than usual, as if it were making a special effort to suit her mood. The moon was unnaturally bright, making the grave mounds stand proud – and full – against black shadows; giving the graveyard the look of an old black and white horror movie. The lopsided rows of grave-stones looked like giant teeth and the shadows behind them suggested anything could be lurking out there, looking up at her window.

The clock by her bed told her it was just gone 3am, yet the heat was still oppressive and her head throb-bed. She was very thirsty.

Downstairs, Elgar got up from his bed and rushed over to her, huffing and bouncing.

'Elgar!' Her father's voice came from the living room, sounding gravely and harsh, as if he hadn't used it in a while. Nancy hadn't noticed he was still up as she came downstairs, but her father now opened the door a few inches and she could see a dim table lamp throwing out a yellowish oval of light onto one of her mother's small tables. Her dad was holding a glass in his hand. He had his pyjamas on. 'What's wrong with you? Bloody dog … ' Her father made to get up as Nancy –

she didn't quite know why – slipped behind the door. Elgar looked briefly crestfallen, shot Nancy a regretful look and went back to his basket.

Her father shook his head and sank back into the armchair, pushing the door closed.

The following morning, her father had already gone when Nancy came downstairs for breakfast. With bright sunlight streaming through the window, her mother had seemed in a better mood – positively cheerful in fact. 'Another beautiful day!' she trilled as the dog, picking up on the good vibe, wiggled around the kitchen, his tail thumping, randomly bumping into furniture.

Shortly afterwards, Nancy headed off in the direction of the library where she spent a fruitless hour looking at books on local history, hoping that she would find something about those stones in there or – even though it was a long-shot – something about the boy: a local interest story about apparitions ... or ghosts, perhaps! Eventually, she had to admit she didn't have a clue what she was actually meant to be researching so she closed her book with a bang, making the old lady librarian jump and then frown as Nancy slipped out the double doors.

Taking a narrow alleyway that led from the supermarket into the centre of town, that's when she came across her new friend once more.

'How are your parents?' he asked it with so much sincerity, a frank look of concern and genuine warmth in his grey eyes that Nancy nearly blurted out the whole truth about her mother, the baby, money worries and about none of them getting on lately. However, she was old enough to know now that when people asked how you or your family were – especially people one didn't know very well – they rarely, if ever, expected an honest answer.

'Fine, thanks,' she said briskly and, to change the subject, she made a point of staring closely at Buk's parchment.

Buk followed her gaze with a look of vague amusement on his face. 'It's getting hotter,' he remarked.

Nancy looked up. 'Yeah, the papers say we're in for the worst heat wave for thirty years.' She squinted up at the sun. 'Forget Global Warming – this is more like Global Frying.'

'Ha,' said Buk but he didn't exactly smile. He turned his parchment flat, running his fingers lightly over the surface. Nancy watched fascinated as the words parted beneath the tips of his fingers, shimmering liquid crystal, like the surface of molten lead being disturbed.

'You're really going to have to tell me where I can get one of those. Does it send emails?'

Buk did not answer. 'The world is slowing … I'm getting tired … the words …,' he paused and sighed, then frowned, 'the words on the Codice seem to be getting *stuck*.' He looked at the parchment – the thing he called a Codice. 'At least, they don't seem to move like they used to … I think this is why everywhere is getting so hot. If the Codice stops working that will be the end of everything … ,' he trailed off.

Nancy looked up and saw some older girls she knew vaguely from school sitting outside Starbucks. All boots and hair. 'Whatever do you mean?' she asked.

Buk met Nancy's eye and not for the last time she felt uncomfortable and somehow extraordinary under his young, yet old gaze.

'Let me show you something,' he said.

Chapter 6

A s the extraordinary boy with ash hair stood up, he took hold of her hand ever so gently. And that was all it required.

It was one of those unexpected moments when life seemed to freeze-frame. If Nancy had been looking at the scene through the lens of a webcam, she would have assumed that her laptop had just crashed. All noise around her abated and all the people, cars and buses stopped dead. Buk and Nancy now stood in their own bubble of space and time.

'Hold this,' he said offering her a corner of the Codice. 'And look very carefully at this symbol here.'

Immediately as Nancy took the Codice, she felt a strange sensation up her arms and between her eyes. The Codice felt warm and soft, like skin. 'It's alive!' she exclaimed in sudden realisation.

'Shh,' said Buk. 'Just concentrate.'

Nancy looked where he was pointing and saw a letter, similar to an 'Ω', about halfway down the page. It reminded her of a gate. She felt a bit silly at first but the longer she looked at the letter on the page, the less self-conscious she felt and the more absorbed. The letter retreated, as the page around it grew larger until it filled her field of vision.

She was standing in front of a large door a few inches from her nose and the door became a question.

'What's just happened?' She could tell Buk was trying not to look too pleased with himself.

'Push it,' he said.

Feeling like Alice, she gave the door a tentative prod.

It didn't budge.

Buk smiled. 'It's quite heavy.'

'OK!' Nancy gave the newly appeared door a whole-hearted shove and it swung open with a rush of vaguely familiar mulchy smells, revealing the same wooded path she had walked along in her dream from a few nights ago. A gentle gust of warm, wet air blew on her face and stirred her fringe just as she realised that there was never any wind in dreams. Apart from that, the scene before her was identical – the dark green light, the huge, ancient trees, the creepers and the moss that hung everywhere. Through the branches, she could see the gentle dip and sweep of a valley where tall grass grew, interspersed with bright red poppies. There were no hedgerows, or fences and no sign of any road nor, indeed, any human habitation. She stepped forward as Buk followed just behind her and heard the door swing shut with a satisfying thunk, much like their front door at home. 'Where are we?'

'We haven't moved,' replied the boy and he pointed at the small stone he had been sitting on – now no longer poking out of the tarmac but rooted, instead, to the forest floor of moss and leaf.

'So, this is Henley? I don't think much of the shops.'

'This is how it once was. Then the whole world was called *Jannat Adn* ... or something like that anyway.'

'This isn't some sort of virtual reality thingy is it? A really advanced one?' She paused then gave him a narrow look. 'Or have you drugged me?'

'No, Nancy. It is just a very long time ago.'

And it wasn't until later that Nancy realised that she had never told him her name.

For now, she was mesmerised: she looked at her surroundings, before asking, 'how long?'

'Oh, millions of years ago,' said Buk off-handedly, apparently completely unaware that the colour had just drained from Nancy's face. He was actually peering through the haze at something on the horizon.

At the news they had apparently just jumped back in time, Nancy immediately felt hot, then cold, then a bit wobbly. She couldn't quite decide whether she should be incredibly excited or sick. She got around the problem by pretending it wasn't really happening to her.

'Look!' cried Buk – his delight cutting through her confusion. He pointed through the trees, out into the savannah where a river – presumably the Thames – flowed and three or four brightly coloured birds flapped in a leisurely way along the valley. Their chest plumage was a smart show of green and gold but, as the sun caught the darker feathers on the wing, it burst into a rainbow pattern of colours. Their bills were huge and very pointed. Even from a distance, Nancy could see that the upper and lower beaks were filled with hundreds of razor-like teeth. As they came closer, several shadows fell across the forest floor and Nancy realised that these birds were enormous. Closer to the size of light aircraft.

'Those are Pterodactyls!' she exclaimed. They'd done the National History Museum just before Christmas.

'I don't know,' replied Buk, 'they used to be called Tark – they're a species long dead. Now these ... ,' he said breaking off abruptly, looking excited and, at the same time, respectful, 'are still around in your day. They've been here almost as long as me.' Nancy looked. At first she couldn't see anything at all, but just then something flitted into a single shaft of light that shone through the lattice work of branches and leaves hundreds of feet above. Nancy had a brief vision of dragonfly wings and stunningly beautiful features.

'What … ?'

'A Vykolakas,' interrupted Buk, 'and he's pleased to meet you – says humans have obviously come on a long way.' The small, yet exquisite creature flicked his wings and shot upwards, following the beam of sunlight, like a lift, all the way to the roof of the forest. Nancy turned her attention back to the familiar-ish looking river.

All along the bank, huge flowers draped their heads, nodding in the tropical breeze, their thick stems bending under the weight of electric blue and blood-red displays of giant petals.

'My mother would die on the spot with happiness if she saw those,' remarked Nancy and then squealed. '*What the* … ?' The whole forest floor had just lifted up four inches and crashed down again, like a giant plate being dropped. There was a short pause and then another crash made the whole forest shake again, though far worse this time. Nancy heard branches splitting as something enormous moved through the woods towards them. A gnarled pair of calloused knuckles and hairy fingers, as fat as pig bellies, pushed through the undergrowth. The head that followed was essentially human, though lumpy and mis-shapen. Sagging purple lips and a forehead as wide as the side of a house protruded in two rocky overhangs topped with thick black bristles. He was dribbling and, as he hummed to himself, a stream of saliva landed in gloopy splashes at his horribly dirty feet.

He was incredibly hairy, which was a blessing because he didn't appear to Nancy to be wearing anything at all.

The troll showed no particular sign of having noticed the two children as he stomped past, crashing his way deeper into the forest.

'Pooh,' remarked Nancy, wrinkling her nose.

'Hmm, yes,' agreed Buk, mildly. 'It's been a long time. I'd forgotten about that.'

Once she'd got over her squeamishness about personal hygiene, Nancy was intrigued. 'I thought they never existed?'

Buk looked perplexed. 'What, them?' he said pointing in the rough direction of the large dent the troll had left in the woods when he'd lumbered through.

'Er, yes, otherwise we'd have seen bones, fossils, that sort of thing. In museums.'

Buk shook his head. 'It doesn't work like that … the stories are just as important as collections of old bones … their bones aren't like ours.'

'What do you mean?'

'The trolls may have been big, but they weren't strong. Not like ... ', he gestured vaguely at the trees, ' ... the Vykolakas.'

'Yes, but what did you mean by *stories are just as important as bones*?' Nancy was beginning to realise that there was no such thing as an easy conversation as far as Buk was concerned but, somehow, he was still better company than anyone she knew lately.

'Everyone has heard of trolls in the tales that humans have passed on over generations. It's like dragons – these are just humans remembering the last of the great dinosaurs. Anyway, troll bones are very brittle, they're big but not that strong, which is partly why they died out so soon after now – I mean – *here*,' he frowned, ' ... or perhaps, I mean *then*,' he shook his head, ' ... anyway their bones usually dry up and crumble to nothing except the large piles of chalk you still see on hills sometimes – so, you see, nothing remains but the legends, which is why they're so important.'

'Oh,' said Nancy who found she had a lot to think about. Pretending to stare at the river, she studied Buk out of the corner of her eye and saw that he seemed to be younger and somehow healthier looking than he had been before they had come here. She wondered why that was. She waved her hand at the forest around them. 'Why are you showing me this?'

'I want you to understand.'

'Understand what?'

'What really matters, of course.'

Chapter 7

And the weather just got hotter.

A day after her *adventure* with Buk, Nancy was down by the river again – this time by the rowing club, dangling her bare feet and legs in the Thames, which, in the last few weeks, had become low and sluggish with lack of rain. Even the willows that lined the river from St Mary's Church to Marsh Lock looked as exhausted as Nancy felt these days. A group of boys kicked a ball around in the middle of the park, but most people just flopped about on the grass, dozing with books or t-shirts over their heads. It all looked rather messy.

Nancy's head still throbbed vaguely and she had an empty feeling in her stomach but no appetite.

She had woken up in the morning, excited by what Buk had shown her and feeling somehow more positive than she had been in ages.

The magic and the mystery, she thought, trying out irony ... but it *was* exciting. And it felt great to feel something for a change other than being cross all the time – or scared.

However, on the way to the bathroom she had come to a sudden stop on the landing. Drifting up the stairwell she could hear the sound of her mother crying. Her father was doing his best to comfort her but, although his intentions were probably good, he wasn't making a very good job of it.

'I'm sick with worry ... *mumble mumble*,' (Nancy assumed her father was hugging her mother at that precise moment). 'Every day I try and try but I get nothing ... it's like she's switched off at the mains ..., she won't communicate ... I put food out for her ... it's ridiculous.'

What?! Nancy couldn't believe her ears – were they talking about her? *The nerve of it!* At first she had assumed it would be something about the Mole-hill, or money, or her dad staying up late drinking too much of that disgusting cheap whisky he bought from the local supermarket. God, *honestly*, they had enough on their plate without picking on her ...

Nancy flung her wash things to one side and flew down the stairs in a rage, bursting into the kitchen mid-flow. ' ... I can't believe you two, you should be worrying about that!' she took a step back and pointed dramatically at the Molehill, 'or about having a car that keeps breaking down or a house that's freezing in the winter 'cos the heating's only on for an hour a day or … *or* any one of a hundred things, not *me* – I'm the least of your worries!'

At that point it all became too much for Elgar – evidently being a dog who liked to avoid confrontation – and he started bouncing clumsily up and down on his front paws, barking then trying to jump up at Nancy who was still glaring at her parents, and who was probably by now all red and furious and slightly mad looking.

As usual, her father stooped to the occasion and ducked the main issue. 'Would you stop that bloody dog barking for two minutes, what's wrong with it?' For a second he looked like he was actually going to kick Elgar, then he simply grabbed his bag full of music scores and his ancient laptop and marched out of the kitchen. Nancy's dad was a big, bear-like man – more like a rugby player than someone who earned his living waving a chopstick about. So large, he actually had to stoop slightly to get through the front door and, as he did so, he paused and looked back at them, still half angry, half guilty. 'I've really *got* to go to work … I'm sorry.' At least he had the decency not to slam the door.

Nancy's Mum blew her nose, raised an eyebrow and sighed as if to say, *men!*

Back in his basket, Elgar humphed too; as if to say, *humans!*

And so later, sitting by the river, Nancy turned her thoughts away from the argument that morning and thought about Buk – to take her mind off things at home. The day before had seemed so bizarre that she had deep-seated personal reasons for believing none of it was real. But so what? It felt better than everything at home.

Before they had left the forest, Buk had fished his magic Codice thingy out of his pocket and had started reading from it.

'You don't say much,' remarked Nancy after a bit.

'No, not unless it improves on silence.'

Looking over his shoulder, the words were more lively than she'd seen them before, so perhaps he was right, it did appear to be working better now. The characters on the Codice also seemed less well formed, more childish but the Codice itself positively hummed with life.

She looked up as it became apparent that (somehow!) they were now standing on the balcony of a white tower, looking out over the rainforest. Her arms felt odd and when she looked down she saw she was wearing a long silk gown, just like the fairytale princess dresses she had worn at parties when she was much younger, and tiny satin slippers that sparkled at the ends with what looked like crushed rubies of all things. She wrinkled her nose – as hallucinations went, this was getting corny. Then again, Nancy couldn't help turning her ankle to admire the shoes.

Buk read on, seemingly oblivious to the fact their immediate environment had just, completely inexplicably, changed. Now he started to recite, but none of his words made any sense to her, or rather, he made a curious keening noise in the back of his throat that quickly became hypnotic and the sounds rolled into one, more like a strange type of music than anything else.

'This is Legend,' he breathed.

Gradually at first, then faster, the light in the forest around them dimmed from dark green to grey and tiny silver dots began to appear in the sky. Very soon it became very dark in the forest, as the number of stars multiplied from hundreds to thousands of minute pinpricks of light. It looked very much as if someone had thrown handfuls of small, sharp diamonds across a vast black velvet sheet and Nancy stared in wonder, now only dimly aware of Buk's song. She had never seen so many stars in the night sky at home, nor ones that shone even half as bright. Everything in this place, even the heavens, looked new and fresh and somehow more *in focus*.

Buk's song changed in tempo and continued. There was something joyful about it, but infinitely complex: as if he had gathered up all the best bits of music and writing she had ever heard or read and translated it into this strange language, set to a looping rhythm.

Then a few of the stars seemed to expand, until she began to make them out more clearly as actual planets. One burned so obviously crimson in the night sky that it must have been Mars. Another quickly distinguished itself by having rings, so it was probably Saturn. The largest seemed cloudy and troubled, swathed in a great coloured eiderdown of billowing gas – Jupiter.

Buk's song continued, becoming more insistent, like a chorus and the planets began to move across the night sky.

Then the other stars, the red dwarfs, gas giants and suns, all millions of light years away, began to revolve too and the forest about them disappeared.

Snow dusted the bare earth around them and a sheet of ice began to spread across the countryside in the distance, coming to a stop at the edge of the frozen river below them.

Buk's words billowed in the frozen air and Nancy began to feel numb with cold.

The song changed once again and became faster as gradually the ice retreated and the area around them was replaced with a new kind of forest filled with more familiar trees and plants. The river swelled and houses appeared. As they did so, the planets seemed to retreat back into anonymity and the night sky turned from grey to light blue.

Buk's song was sad now and immeasurably more true and beautiful for it. Slowly the sun rose and Buk, eventually, stopped.

They were back in the town, the tower was gone and so too the beautiful dress.

He sighed. 'There are no more words,' he said and Nancy noticed that the Codice now hung limp in his hands, the page empty of words, the surface brittle.

Nancy was confused. 'What's happening?'

For a moment it looked like Buk would not reply. He seemed exhausted. Then he licked his dry lips. 'It's all the same ... but I only just noticed,' was what he said.

Chapter 8

Vast, black clouds moved across the twilight sky, looking polluted and menacing: as if they were being belched out from some immense, soot-ridden factory just over the horizon.

'Storm comin', I'd say,' muttered Nancy's mum, as she marched across Nancy's bedroom and closed the sash window with some difficulty. Her hair had gone static and flyaway in the last hour – more so than usual – which was a sure sign that the weather was about to change. Being an artist, Nancy had always wondered if her mother was not super-sensitive to these things. Her normally slightly eccentric, scatty-looking hair would go limp and reddish if it rained for more than a week. However, if the weather was getting better it would resume its strawberry-blond bounciness, moving independently of its owner as she bustled around her studio. Flecks of paint at the ends just added to the effect.

'Five hundred years ago, my wife would probably have been burnt for being a witch!' her dad once joked over drinks with the neighbours.

'Hah hah hah,' replied Mr. and Mrs. Jonathan McCully without any trace of humour whatsoever, both looking into their glasses. The McCullys built websites from home for a living and sold timeshares in Portugal on the side. Nancy had no idea what a timeshare was, but she just bet it was as boring as working on a computer all day in the spare room.

⁂

In the end the storm never materialised, so eventually Nancy got up and opened the window again, to get the benefit of what little air there was.

She sat on her bed for a long while, wondering if what Buk had said was true. Had the world *really* stopped turning for some reason, was that why it was getting hotter every day? It seemed distinctly unlikely, but so did time travel and (apparently) Buk had managed to pull that off without too much difficulty – sixty million years – all between breakfast and lunch. But why would the world stop revolving because of the stories, or the words on the Codice? Whichever way you looked at it – *that* was highly suspect. And anyway, the government and their armies of geeks – who kept pens in their top pockets – would have noticed and they'd all be falling over themselves to do something about it.

Or perhaps they *had* noticed and this was all a big cover up – *da da daaah?*

But Nancy shook her head. She enjoyed conspiracy stories as much as anyone – gleefully trading rumours with friends at school about government assassinations, dead aliens found in the desert and fake moon landings; but that didn't seem to fit here somehow, and yet nor did it seem right that Buk was playing a trick on her. He just didn't seem *like* that. But all that fairytale stuff: the romantic tower, the dress, *those shoes* … she didn't swallow either … . Whatever. And the Codice. One thing she was sure about was that Buk was worried – he believed in It and this should have made him seem ridiculous but instead it made her feel sorry for him.

She tried googling *Buk* and *Codice* and *world revolving* and got absolutely nowhere. After ten minutes or so she closed her laptop and went upstairs to watch her mother work.

Mum usually didn't mind, as long as she didn't fidget or talk to friends on her mobile.

~

Upstairs, the light coming in through the round window had a sort of heavenly brightness to it on account of the sun reflecting off the bruised storm clouds that were now retreating towards Reading. Nancy's mum was making the most of the weird light; slopping paint onto a large canvass and singing along with the radio that was tuned to a local station playing old hits from the 80's. Her dad would have had a seizure if he caught her listening to this.

Nancy smiled to herself and sat down on an old beanbag in the corner. As she did so a cloud of dust erupted, making her sneeze. Nancy's mother, up until now engrossed in what she had been doing, jumped and looked around.

'Sorry,' said Nancy meekly and, because she didn't want to get kicked out, she made a show of reading the front cover of yesterday's newspaper that was lying there.

Apart from a small piece about the president of Hungary visiting the prime minister, it was all about the heatwave. The paper was one of the big national dailies and it had obviously decided to take an inter-national perspective on the crisis. Nancy read with growing alarm that the problem really did seem to be global: in America – especially in some of the hotter places like Florida or California – there had been fires and panic buying in several places, with rich people filling their garages with stacks of mineral water, tinned fruit and survival kits. In LA, a lot of big houses belonging to important people had then been raided by other, poorer, people in order to steal the carefully stocked supplies and this had meant that sales of guns had gone up. It was only a matter of time, predicted the reporter ominously, before someone got themselves shot over water!

And things closer to home were not much better – although perhaps a little weirder – bottled water had also run out in most shops in Britain and a lot of families living in the countryside had opened up old wells or had started to pump water from nearby rivers to use in the garden. In suburbia the police had been kept busy dealing with hundreds of neighbours reporting each other for improper use of hosepipes. French air traffic controllers had gone on strike for some reason and in Germany a sausage factory had to close down when the sausages kept exploding in the heat.

'A giant exploding black pudding ist no laffing matter!' a visibly-upset general manager [pictured] insisted.

More seriously, and perhaps because of the foreign president's visit, the lead story showed a picture of the old town centre in Budapest. The thatched roof belonging to a famous restaurant had caught light the day before and half of the main square had gone up in flames in a matter of an hour or so. Were it not for the quick action of the fire fighters in spraying the area with water from helicopters, the whole medieval square would now be ash and rubble. *The day before.*

Nancy quickly double-checked the date on the newspaper. Twenty-four hours ago, whilst the fire had been raging four hundred miles away, she had been with Buk in the forest.

She looked carefully at the newspaper. The photo they had printed right across the top of the page was a dramatic shot of three Hungarian fire fighters directing a powerful-looking hose at a large, gabled building. Smoke and flame took up at least half the shot.

She stared at the picture for a long time – just to make sure.

In the extreme edge of the photograph, sitting on a stone, very similar to the one in the Marketplace, was a solitary, almost forlorn figure. He was half-obscured by thick smoke, perilously close to the flames but seemingly ignored by the men fighting to save the building. There was no doubt about it.

It was Buk.

Chapter 9

Before she had time to think about what it all meant, her attention was ripped away by a sudden, almost animal cry, from her mother.

Dropping the newspaper, Nancy spun around just in time to see her bend double and fall to her knees. The paintbrush in her hand dropped to the floor as she clasped her belly, then her mother's shoulder knocked the easel sideways, tipping the half-finished painting and a livid rainbow of paint into the centre of the room.

'Just stay there Mum – don't try and move!' Nancy narrowly avoided the falling canvass as she ran for the stairs, down to the landing where the upstairs phone usually sat on a marble-topped table.

The cradle was empty, a flashing green light showed it was picking up a signal. Nancy was just about to run down to the kitchen where the other cordless was kept when she heard the phone go *click* and her mother's voice saying, '*Aargh*, sorry, yes, ambulance … '

As she raced back up the stairs, Nancy realised her mother must have had the phone in her apron pocket whilst she worked. 'Oh, one, four, nine, one … four double one, double six … seven … two … my name? Dorothy Prentice … pee, ar, ee, yes, that's it … one, two, nine St Andrei Road, RG9 1AA … for me … I think I might be having a baby … it'll be six weeks early … aah aaah … sorry, yes I'm fine to carry on … but can you send someone … aagghhh!'

Nancy burst back into the room just as her mother clicked the off button on the phone and lay back down on the dusty floor. Her forehead was beaded with sweat and she had gone almost the same colour as the white linen smock she always wore under her apron when painting. Nancy laid a hand on her shoulder and smoothed her hair back. 'It's OK,' she said. 'Just take deep breaths.' For a few moments her mother's eyes were staring and blank, then gradually they seemed to focus in on Nancy's face as her breathing became more even.

'Oh!' she said, almost as if surprised and then she smiled and closed her eyes.

Exactly nine minutes later two green-clad ambulance people came tentatively through the front door that Nancy had left open.

'I'm up here!' shouted her mother. 'Actually I'm feeling much better,' she said to the young, rather sweet-looking lady ambulance driver when they had got all the way up the stairs. 'It was probably just a twinge. This is my second. I'm not due for nearly another two months!'

The paramedic nodded and made a sympathetic noise as she finished taking her mum's blood pressure and looked at her colleague.

She then spent a few moments gently feeling her mother's stomach before saying, 'Well, normally there would be nothing to get worked up about, but your blood pressure *is* very high, so we'll have to take you in. It'll be another night in hospital, I'm afraid, Mrs Prentice.'

Nancy's mum looked rueful. 'Thought so,' she said.

⁂

The ambulance ride was less exciting and a lot more uncomfortable than Nancy had imagined it would be. Whilst her mother chatted to the nice ambulance lady, who turned out to be a proper doctor doing some volunteer work, Nancy tried her best not to fall off the narrow seat at the back each time they went around a corner. Once, during a bit of especially heavy traffic on the Oxford ring road, they had put the siren on. And that had just made it noisy *and* uncomfortable.

The fact that Nancy was feeling a bit carsick by the time they got there had something to do with the twisty ride but, she had to admit, it also had a lot to do with the prospect of actually going into the hospital.

What was she so afraid of? What was inside that place?

A small, shrill voice in her head reasoned that if her mother was ill, she might lose the baby.

A tight ball of acid in the pit of her stomach made her feel properly sick and by the time they pulled up outside A&E her knees felt wobbly. She kept telling herself that it was only a big building, just like any other, where people went to work everyday. It even had shops and a Starbucks or two.

However, by the time they had managed to gently manoeuvre her mother out of the ambulance and into a wheelchair, Nancy felt so generally crap she was only vaguely aware of her father arriving. He rushed up, past Nancy, and grabbed his wife's hand. 'I got your text. Is everything alright?' He looked at the driver who nodded reassuringly.

As they got to the sliding doors, Nancy did her best to follow but by now she was in the midst of full-blown panic attack. She could hear blood rushing in her head and she was quite sure she was about to faint or be sick or do both.

The sliding doors parted to allow her mother and her father to disappear into the hospital with the Molehill and Nancy caught the cool antiseptic and floor wax smell of the reception and almost gagged. She tried to steel herself to go in, but the feeling of animal fear simply grew worse. She marched up to the door several times, each time stopping just short of the threshold. Eventually she gave up.

Nancy sat down heavily on the hot concrete outside the hospital and burst into tears. And, the really stupid thing was, she had no idea why.

But that didn't make her feel any better.

Chapter 10

Red and silver lights, the grinding then tearing sound of metal on metal ...

She forced herself awake, struggling up through the bed sheets, gasping, like a drowning swimmer fighting a desperate battle for air. She was drenched in sweat.

The house was quiet as a vault, which was not surprising as Nancy was quite alone – her dad had stayed at the hospital and even Elgar had been collected by her aunt who lived in Reading. Nancy supposed that she should have gone too but she made what she thought was a clever pre-emptive strike and texted from the bus on her way back from hospital to say she was staying with Millie.

She was beginning to regret that decision now as she lay in bed, listening to the movement of the house, each familiar knock, tap or creak causing her to relax somewhat until a sudden, unfamiliar noise would make her stiffen in her own bed. She had always hated the dark and she generally slept with the curtains open to let in the light from the street below.

That evening, however, the familiar, orange glow of the street lamp was absent – it was probably broken – and the only light coming through the open window was a cold, silver reflection off the moon, falling across her bed in a long strip; like the start of a ghost road, leading out into the cemetery beyond. The boiler in the kitchen made a low snickering noise quite unlike anything it had ever uttered before and suddenly each shadowy alcove in her room seemed to contain a threat: to conceal unpleasant, malevolent things.

She knew, from past experience, that the longer she lay still, the worse the fear of the dark unknown would become; so with some effort she forced herself upright, swinging her bare feet onto the cool floorboards by her bed.

Drawn by the light of the moon, she padded silently towards her window. Outside, the cemetery was lit in black and white as before and the dried grass between the stones looked coarse and matted, reminding Nancy of the troll's hair. At the far edge stood some very old trees whose boughs formed a canopy, like an awning, that overhung the wall, marking the start of where the oldest graves had been dug. These decrepit tombs congregated hap-haphazardly, leaning in on one another, almost as if the pitted statues of dubious angels that topped the vaults had gathered the dead closer – the better to whisper secrets to one another at night.

Shrouded in the shadows made by the ancient, twisted trees, stood a solitary figure.

Looking directly up at Nancy.

As if she were sleepwalking, Nancy turned away from the window and walked towards the stairs. She didn't notice the dark shapes that gathered at her back as she crept down the stairs and silently crossed the hall. The kitchen was lit in harsh lines too and she was able to locate the backdoors keys in the tub easily.

Opening the door, she stepped out into the cool, quiet night, leaving it open, without a backward glance. At the end of their garden a small door, with the remnants of green paint peeling from the old woodwork, had been cut into the back wall. It led directly into the other world of the cemetery and, although it was usually firmly bolted from the inside, Nancy wasn't in the least surprised to find it half open. She pushed through the ivy and briars, hardly minding the thorns that scratched her bare arms and snagged on her white night dress.

Buk stood on the other side of the door, waiting for her.

Even in the poor light, Nancy was shocked by how different he looked now. Earlier, in the prehistoric world, his features had become animated and his eyes caught the light and sparkled. He had been brimming with boyish energy. Now, and it may or may not have been the moonlight, he was the same colour as the stones that surrounded him and he hunched, almost like an old man.

'Good evening, Nancy,' he said gravely and held up the Codice. Wordlessly she took it and stared at the shifting runes and symbols.

This time it was much easier …

Nancy chose a letter at random, shaped like a tree and, before long she had the now-familiar sense of blind vertigo, like standing on the edge of a sharp drop in thick fog, before a gentle push from Buk had her falling down a smooth, spiralling tunnel … and then out into daylight.

Chapter 11

S he found herself standing in the middle of an elegantly laid out garden. Nancy looked about but saw no sign of Buk this time, although a linnet on a nearby tree appeared to be watching her more closely than was strictly normal for a bird.

The very same wall that had screened the graves now stood to her left, although the trees were older and unfamiliar.

It was summer in the garden, too, but cooler than wherever or perhaps more accurately, *whenever* home was. And all around her were children playing in the long grass. Their laughter was comforting, reminding Nancy, with a slight sense of longing, of a time – not long passed – when she was completely contented to have a few friends around to play in the back garden.

Unsure what to do next, she just stood there and drank the scene in. She felt something brush her fingertips and Nancy looked down to see a very small boy smiling up at her. Instinctively, she took him by his plump, soft hand and allowed him to lead her to a group of children who were starting a game of tag.

At first, she felt self-conscious and clumsy. But the children's enthusiasm was infectious and she found herself laughing as excitedly as them as they ran from one temporary hiding place to the next.

However, a booming voice from the gate clubbed the laughter to terrified silence. 'OUT, OUT, GET OUT OF MY GARDEN, OR I WILL STOMP ON YOU!'

The children ran as the linnet circled Nancy's head crying out loudly, the bird's wings flicking her face when it came too close.

The giant caught sight of Nancy amidst the children who fled over the wall and he roared in anger.

Nancy desperately looked around for the smallest boy who had taken her hand, but the scene went dark and all sound was abruptly cut off.

She stood there in the pitch black, with a mounting sense of panic at being stranded in this dark, unknown place. It started to spread with a tight knot in her throat and shortness of breath.

Just as it became unbearable and she was about to cry out, a smear of light appeared in the distance.

It grew steadily larger until she could make out the trees and the walls and the large house belonging to the giant again. She hadn't moved but her feet had just gone numb.

Nancy looked down to find out why and saw that she was standing ankle deep in snow. The realisation just made her feel even colder and she wrapped her bare arms around her body to try and keep some heat in.

Over the wall, outside the garden, she could hear children playing in the street, but their games were subdued and there seemed little or none of the joy left in their voices that there had been before.

Nancy looked back at the silent house. All the windows had been boarded up except one on the ground floor that was open. It appeared gloomy and cold, like a grudging invitation. She crept over and peered in carefully, seeing a bare room with peeling wallpaper and an empty hearth where no fire seemed to have been lit for years. On a stool, in the middle of the room, sat the giant. She stared in at him for a few minutes, her fear giving way to compassion. She had never seen someone look quite so lonely.

Knowing just what she had to do, Nancy walked back across the snow, ignoring the cold that bit through her cotton nightdress, until she came to the large, wrought-iron gate. The heavy latch, shaped like a serpent swallowing its own tail, was rusted and took some shifting.

When she finally managed to release it, she was able to push one half of the gate open with a muffled crunch as it piled up snow in its wake. Then she pulled down a sign saying, **KEPE OWT** that the giant had hastily nailed to a tree.

It took the children in the street a few minutes to realise what Nancy had done. Then, at intervals, faces that were pinched with cold appeared at the opening and sneaked looks in.

'Don't be afraid,' said Nancy as warmly as possible. She clearly wasn't a giant and she didn't look in the least bit angry so, one by one, they tiptoed across the snow towards the trees where the linnet watched the proceedings closely from a bare branch.

The instant they entered the garden, the snow began to melt and flowers sprung out of the grass in abundance, as if they had been expecting the rush of small feet that tore across the grass. Within minutes the whole garden had come alive with green shoots and bursts of colour.

With a crash, the front door of the house was flung open and the giant, dressed in an old brown dressing gown and muffler, came outside. Everyone stopped playing and looked afraid. But instead of shouting at them, he was laughing, his cliff-like face creasing in strange ways that suggested smiling wasn't one of his regular habits. And Nancy laughed too, looking about her at the children she recognised playing in the lush grass.

However, in one corner of the garden winter stubbornly remained.

At the foot of an apple tree stood the smallest child, the one who had taken Nancy's hand. He was crying because he couldn't reach the branches to climb up.

The giant had noticed this too and he strode across the garden, his face grim. Nancy held her breath.

Then, with the greatest of care, he knelt down, took the small boy in one of his huge hands and placed him on a low bough of the tree. Instantly, the tree sprang into pure white apple blossom. The boy stopped crying and looked at the giant with large eyes. Then he looked towards Nancy and smiled.

~

Nancy stayed there for a very long time, watching over the garden with the linnet.

She saw the seasons change outside the high walls, but in the garden itself eternal summer reigned. Years passed and the giant grew old, content to spend his days sitting on a bench watching the delighted children play.

From time to time, though, he looked sad and Nancy knew why: ever since that first day, when summer had returned to the garden, the small boy had not come back to play, and his tree remained empty of small children, bare of leaves and forlorn.

She remembered the feel of his hand and the look of forgiveness on his small face and she understood the giant's sense of longing.

Then one day, very early in the morning, she heard the linnet call sharply from the gate. The giant heard it too and he came out of the house. In the corner of the garden, where the empty tree stood, a small bundle lay on the ground. All around the base of the tree was a thin covering of snow and Nancy saw bright spots staining it red.

Both the giant and Nancy ran across the lawn towards the small boy.

'WHO HAS DONE THIS TOO YOU?' stormed the giant, staring at the wounds in the palms of boy's hands and at the holes in his feet.

She felt the giant's towering fury too! Who would harm such a small child? Who *could*? She thought of her feelings towards the Molehill and her outrage was suddenly sliced through with cold, sharp guilt. The spots of blood reminded her of the studio at the top of their house.

But the child just looked up at the giant and shook his head. 'No-one has done this to me – these are wounds of love: all parents carry them for their children. You welcomed me in your garden, it's time you came to mine.'

When the other children arrived, they found the old giant lying peacefully under the tree covered with white blossom.

Nancy was stood close by crying for her dead friend and for her own sense of selfishness, when her parents had much more to worry about than her.

Then the linnet sang one brief note and swooped down from the tree. It landed on her shoulder, hardly any weight at all, and suddenly she was back in the cemetery.

Chapter 12

There wasn't even a ruddy pier at Little-hampton!

Instead, a long promenade went from the posh coffee shops and nice hotels at one end, all the way to the crumbling amusement arcade and stalls selling dead fishy *things* in little white tubs of jelly at the other.

It was barely a week after Buk had visited Nancy in the cemetery and she now sat on a bench a hundred miles away – very much in the real world – looking out at the people lounging on the beach and wondering if she should get two or, indeed, perhaps even three tattoos.

As soon as her mother had got out of hospital in Oxford, her father had packed their things into the old Volvo – leaving almost no space at the back for Nancy, who squeezed in next to the folding chairs and windbreak, and sulked the whole way there.

Her father had mostly grown up in Littlehampton. When his parents died in a plane crash on their way to Paris just after the war, the young John Prentice had been sent to live with two doting but very elderly and old-fashioned aunts who liked nothing more than bracing walks, tepid cups of sweat tea on the beach front, stray cats and opera. Dodgy hot beverages aside, her dad had inherited their love of music and an almost pathological fondness for the town and so he packed Nancy and her mum off there whenever he thought they all needed cheering up.

In Nancy's view Littlehampton was the most boring resort in the whole of Europe but they really had no money (she had sneaked a look at her father's bank statement on the hall table), so this was the only holiday they were likely to get that year. At least the weather was a bit cooler on the coast.

For the first four days, whilst the fairytale of the selfish giant was fresh in her mind, she found it easy to be nice when she thought of her baby brother, who lay cosseted in her mother's womb – safe and warm and already cared for.

However, as the days drifted by, she began to feel lonely and then resentful all over again. Her parents spent their mornings reading in the garden of the cottage they were renting and their afternoons sitting on the beach or going for short walks into town. And then back again.

Basically though, whichever way she looked at it, they were ignoring her and despite reminding herself that they had other things to worry about, besides Nancy, she couldn't help feeling left out. She told herself that it was all rubbish – that parents didn't simply stop loving one child as soon as another one came along but it didn't help much. Her mother kept calling the hospital too, which was annoying and seemed completely unnecessary.

She also had to admit that partly her feeling the way she did was because her father seemed to have accepted the Molehill in the last week or so. The sea air always made him light-hearted – something she loved when she was small when he took her out fishing – supposedly for mermaids – or hired pedalos and then charged off, frantically peddling them as far out to sea before they got shouted at by her mother to come in.

Once, when Nancy was about eight, he had started building a sandcastle early in the morning. By lunch-time, it was about fifteen feet long and four foot high and he had enlisted the help of half a dozen small boys and girls and even a couple of bored dads. By teatime it was twice the size and by late afternoon, as the tide began to come in, the local paper had sent a reporter down to interview her dad and a photographer to take pictures of what looked like a medieval earthworks on the beach. Hundreds of people had stayed well past their suppertime to watch the huge sand towers, walls and buttresses collapse one by one as the sea came slowly and inexorably in.

Later, standing outside the chip shop, several children had come up and told him it was the best day at the seaside they'd ever had.

She now looked out across the beach and saw him lean over and kiss the Molehill. Her mother smiled and ruffled his hair and Nancy felt like marching over and hitting him on the side of the head. Not wanting the baby was the one thing they used to have in common. She sat there for a while longer, hating herself for being so awful.

She was also worried about Buk. Although she really only hardly knew him – and whether he was real or not – she found she thought about the boy more than any of her friends now.

A day or so after the night he had shown her the selfish giant's story in the cemetery, she had come across him in town, sitting at the bottom of Falaise Square. She watched him for a while, keeping well hidden in the crowds outside a popular restaurant. Nevertheless, she had the distinct impression he knew she was there as, once or twice, he glanced in her direction and half smiled to himself.

From where she sat, he seemed paler and more drawn than ever – his hair now looked completely white, for starters. And the fine china colour of his skin was a sharp contrast to all the well-tanned people who passed him by, oblivious to his presence. Although they were not entirely unaffected by his being there. Nancy noticed how, as each person came close, they seemed to become more animated: silent couples started talking, children skipped, parents smiled as all the while Buk read from his Codice, his lips moving silently, his eyes remaining troubled.

Eventually Nancy went over.

'Hello,' he said, a little solemnly. Even his eyelashes had turned white.

Close up, she was even more shocked by his appearance. His skin was creased, like that of an old man and his eyes were now the dark grey of storm clouds. Shadows formed in the hollows of his cheeks. The Codice still looked wrong, too – somehow dried up and lifeless. Buk saw her staring and pushed it into the fold of his tunic, as if he was hiding a guilty secret.

'Thank you for the other night,' said Nancy, reaching over and touching the back of his hand. It was cold but somehow comforting. She also wanted to say, " yeah, yeah, I get it, I'm just like the selfish giant and I should learn to be nicer to people *just generally* but also *specifically* to my unborn brother but I'm old enough to know the difference between how I *should* feel and how I actually *do* feel and that it's not a simple case of hearing a story to make you do the right thing". But that seemed ungrateful after all the effort he seemed to have gone through.

'The Codice sometimes shows you what it thinks you need to see,' he replied by way of an explanation. 'It's not always welcome.'

'Can you show me another?'

He looked strained and totally worn out. 'I don't know, I'm tired … sorry.'

Chapter 13

A fter nearly a week at Littlehampton, they did Mr Prentice's second favourite thing in the whole world (right after sitting in a chair watching telly).

Mackerel spinning!

They had to get up just after six, but Nancy didn't mind, she had been awake since before five. She'd had another one of her dreams with the noise and rushing lights that she found strangely a lot more disturbing than the excursions to fairytales and legends Buk conjured up for her.

Her mum had decided to stay behind and Nancy was looking forward to spending the day alone with her dad for the first time in months.

On the way to the harbour he'd looked thoughtful at first but as it came into view he started to hum Puccini under his breath, which was a good sign. Nancy slipped her arm in his, pressing the side of her face against his old blue fleece and he gave a vague smile.

As soon as they got onto the boat, he marched down the far end, near the bow and started rummaging around in the bucket of spinning reels.

Nancy decided to leave him alone to enjoy himself and sat on a bench in the stern where she could take in the scenery without getting her hair blown into her mouth. The sea was choppy but in a good way – small, lively looking waves with white frills of foam made the little boat pitch and slap the water as it left the coast behind. Nancy tilted her head back and closed her eyes, enjoying the salt spray and the sun in her face.

She must have drifted off because she opened them with a start when her father plonked a metal bucket down beside her with a clatter. He was grinning from ear to ear. 'That's seven already,' he said. 'I think we're on for a record!'

'Well done.' said Nancy, squinting up at him. 'I'll come and join you in a minute.'

'D'yer want to go owt farther?' asked the skipper, a short man with very white hair and a purplish nose.

'Absolutely!' said her dad, dashing back up to the prow of the boat, like a small boy.

Nancy looked down at the bucket and noticed a small mackerel staring up at her with one eye.

It cleared its throat. ' 'ello.'

Nancy, doing a passable impression of the other fish crowding the bucket, soundlessly opened her mouth and then closed it again. 'Would you like to hear a story?' the mackerel continued.

Nancy hastily gathered her wits. 'Aren't you meant to offer me three wishes or something?'

The mackerel rolled its available eye. 'That's Pollocks.'

'Oh,' said Nancy. 'Sorry.'

'Fink nuffink of it.'

There was a longish pause whilst fish and teenage girl stared at one another. 'Um, I don't mean to pressure you or anything but, thanks to your dad's over-enthusiastic efforts, I've probably only got about ten minutes before I cark it … ' Nancy looked up at her father who was dangling a line in each hand over the side and then at the skipper who was busy staring out at the horizon. Neither seemed to have noticed that there was a talking fish in the boat. She sighed, she *had* been enjoying herself.

'OK, you might as well,' said Nancy. The mackerel, ignoring her tone, seemed to brighten up no end.

'Rightyho, here goes. *Ahem!*:

~

'There was once a fish called Arque.

Arque was a Behemoth – a real miracle of nature and the only one of her kind ever to have existed and she roamed the seas millions of years ago, long before the continents unstuck and the polar caps froze over. She was so large that when she opened her mouth, whales would dart inside and pick at her teeth, like minnows. Each of her fins was a mile long and her tail stretched from one end of the horizon to the other.

'When Arque broke surface just once a year to take a deep bref, the ocean forgot to follow the pull of the Moon and moved its tides, instead, to the pulse of her huge beating heart. Even the stars were awed by her size and she sang to them in the depth of the night, like a mother to her children.

'Her tune was so mournful that one of the stars wept with pity to hear it. Night after night it listened to her slow chant as she traversed the great oceans until the star could bear it no longer.

'It fell to Earth.

'Unfortunately stars just aren't meant to drop out of the sky – Mother Earth is not built for that sort of eventuality and the falling orb of light and rock and terrible heat caused a catastrophe. It punctured the mantel of Earth's crust – the very thing that holds the planet together.

'Now, Arque was not angry at what the foolish star had done – in fact she wept as she raced across the seas to where it had landed – for she knew in her heart that the star had fallen and had died for love of her. But she was alarmed because the sea was now pouring away into the huge hole made by the star. The sea level was dropping dangerously when Arque got there, pulling thousands of fish, crustaceans, coral reefs and underwater habitats into a red and boiling second sea of molten lava below. The first ecological disaster!

'Without hesitation Arque moved her colossal frame over the great hole in the ocean floor and plugged the leak. Just like that.

'Unfortunately, she was now stuck fast.

'She could have thrashed her huge frame from side to side like a salmon on a line but it threatened to cause a tsunami that would swamp the great continent that lay at the heart of the Earth. Arque may have had the power of a small god but she was as gentle as a seahorse.

'So, she waited – patiently watching the sea and the planet slowly evolve around her as thousands of years passed, all the while singing her slow sad tune. After a few tens of millennia, she began to feel drowsy and she closed her eyes. More millennia passed and her skin calcified, slowly turning to a creamy blue rock, like polished marble, as the continents divided and the sea levels dropped, exposing the great sweeping ridge of her back.

'Trees began to grow on her sloping flanks and birds crossed the ocean to sit in them. After a while, mammals arrived too and then 'oomans, who were awestruck at this paradise and called it *Atlantis*.

'At about this time, Arque's song – long-since silenced – had traveled light years through space and a distant species eventually answered her call. They arrived in sleek spaceships and taught the humans living on Atlantis flight, beauty and absolute love. In that order.

'Now they say that lightning never strikes the same place twice, but meteorites must have relatively short memories. After nearly a million years another star fell to Earth in exactly the same spot, shattering Arque into incalculable pieces. Fortunately, the hole beneath her was instantly plugged by the burning rock but thousands of humans and the people from the stars were killed instantly, as well as many species unique to Atlantis – such as the Unicorn and a type of evil-tempered blue parrot.

'As for Arque, a wonderful thing happened, quite unprecedented in the history of any life anywhere: The vast quantities of her shattered remains immediately sprang to life, darting away from where they had spent the last thousand millennia as a huge shoal of silver and blue fish that stretched for thousands of miles.

'And that,' concluded the fish, 'is how the humble mackerel came to be and it is why we still swim in schools, remembering our old form .... thank you for listening.'

The mackerel closed its eye, sighed ... and died.

Chapter 14

It was hardly surprising, then, that Nancy scarcely noticed the rest of the outing pass by. Her dad reached a grand total of seventeen flapping, gulping, silvery-blue mackerel and called it a day. As for Nancy, who'd just lost her taste for fishing, she simply sat in the stern of the boat feeling queasy, wondering if she'd gone mad.

She tried to think rationally about everything that had been happening, as the boat chugged and heaved back to harbour. If Buk was real, then so was the Codice. The Codice had done something very bad to her brain, and now she was imagining things.

Everything considered, she blamed Buk – one hundred percent.

The fact that this time the Codice wasn't anywhere to be seen and yet she'd just had a very real experience of a talking fish, just made everything worse. Worse for Buk, that is. When she caught up with him.

The last day of their holiday passed mercifully without incident, or at least without anything too bizarre happening. Her dad was in the best mood he'd been in for months and even her mother looked much better. 'I told you!' he boomed, kissing Nancy's mother noisily on the cheek over breakfast, 'the sea air will cure anything.' But Nancy hardly slept the final night before they left – her headache had come back and in the early hours, when she finally did drop off, she had another one of her dreams where nothing was clear: just grating metal and light.

When they got home, she found that she was still furious with Buk – so she left the house to find him. It didn't take long. He was sitting in his usual place but his Codice was nowhere to be seen.

He looked at her and yawned. 'Did you have a nice holiday?'

'How did you … ? Never mind that – what have you done to me?'

'I can't do anything to anyone Nancy. I thought you understood that.' For a second she thought he looked sad but then decided it was simply that he looked as tired as she felt.

'I don't believe you. I'm having hallucinations – a fish gave me a bedtime story – what next? Elves in the bathroom? King Arthur popping by for a game of football with my dad? This is all your doing – you and your stupid Codice … it's given me brain damage, it's …'

' … stopped working,' interrupted Buk, looking at his dusty feet.

'What do you mean, *stopped working*?'

'The stories won't come anymore. Without them the Earth will no longer turn. It's already slowing, that's why it's so hot. We need the stories to survive … ' For Nancy that was the last straw.

'What planet are you on?' she yelled – past caring if anyone stared at her. 'The Earth revolves because of the Sun, heatwaves *do* happen,'

Buk, who had been looking at a couple across the street broke off and stared at Nancy intently. 'And how do you know all this?'

'I read it, people told me … '

Buk shrugged imperceptibly. 'Same as me … I read things, I listen to the stories … '

'STORIES! That's all they are.' Nancy pinched the bridge of her nose: her head pounded but she needed to get Buk to see sense. 'It's simple, it really is. Can't you tell the difference between fact and fiction? When people start to imagine they bump into talking fish it's not because fish can talk, it's because they've got a problem … giants don't exist, you can't travel back in time … are you even listening … do you even care?' Buk was staring past her again. She jabbed her finger into his thin chest and felt a brief pang of guilt when she saw pain pass across his face, but her anger wasn't spent yet. 'You can't tell what's real and what's not! My mother's got high blood pressure, she shouldn't be having a baby at her age – there's a good chance she might die ... *that's real* ... and so might the baby!' Nancy shocked herself at that point. It was the first time she had said *baby* out loud and her voice cracked with a raw emotion she'd never felt when she mentioned him before. This just made her even more angry. She wanted to grab the Codice and throw it in the river.

'I only know what's inside my own head,' said Buk, 'same as everyone ...' He looked up at her from where he sat on the small stone. For an instant it looked like he was pleading, the frail face of a boy with the eyes of an old, old man. 'Nancy ... '

But Nancy was walking away.

Chapter 15

❧

S he couldn't care about the heat. She *wouldn't* care about Buk, who sometimes seemed as un-real as the fairytales he immersed her in. And every time she thought about the baby, she simply didn't know what to feel, except a rising sense of panic about what might happen to her mother.

She also knew she should have felt happy that her parents were getting on again, hopeful that her mother hadn't had to go into hospital for two weeks – every passing day making a good birth more likely as the baby developed and grew stronger in her womb.

Instead, she felt somehow transparent – as if she no longer made a proper impression on life around her. Nor it on her. Sitting on her bed all day was the only way she felt anchored. Nancy strongly suspected that if she left the house now, she'd simply blow away in the wind.

But in spite of her best intentions, she did start to feel less angry with Buk. A couple of times she actually got up and went to her desk to write him a letter. Oddly, she wasn't sure if he could even read.

Thinking about her strange friend, in a way she wished that she was him. His understanding of the world seemed simple, less prone to muddles. Stories were easy once you got the hang of them: they had a clear beginning, middle and, most importantly, an end. Also, the ending was nearly always happy – or, at least, even when it wasn't, you usually learnt something useful. The point was stories had a *point* – but she wasn't sure if she could honestly say the same of her own life.

Nothing seemed to have any structure right now, there didn't seem to be a clear beginning, middle nor an end to anything. Perhaps this was what life was really like? Or perhaps if she hurried up and went properly mad she could live in bliss with Buk, happily hopping from one fairy story to the next? Like Disneyland Paris but without the long, boring queues.

Her mother came up most afternoons and sat on her bed with her. Mostly she said nothing but sometimes she talked and Nancy listened, taking comfort more in the sound of her voice than what she actually had to say, most of which was news she already knew anyway.

'Your father is thinking about moving jobs. There's an orchestra in London that's starting up. Not professional musicians, but kids, like you – in age, that is – but not like you, because they all come from broken homes, or are orphans, drug users ... you know. It's got lottery funding and the salary is better than in Oxford, which is not everything, I know but ... well, it would be nice to have some spare money for bits and pieces when the baby comes. I couldn't bear to have to sell the house right now ... '

She went over to the window and looked out at something for a few minutes that Nancy couldn't see.

'Our lawn has dried to nothing,' she remarked. 'The grass looks well and truly dead and I don't think some of those shrubs your grandmother bought us when we moved in are coming back next year. More like *hardly perennials*.' She turned back to Nancy and gave a stagey grin, before sitting back down on the end of the bed. 'The baby seems fine, I'm fine ... not that that matters ... '

As her mother got up to go, she pressed a red button at the head of Nancy's bed that she'd never noticed before. Somewhere down the corridor, outside her bedroom, she heard footsteps on a polished floor.

Chapter 16

Nancy woke up a few hours later, coming to slowly at first, then with an abrupt jolt when she realised there was a face very close to her own.

Buk was grinning at her and holding his Codice up. 'Heeelllloooo', he rocked forward on the balls of his feet, nearly bumping noses with her.

'Buk?... *Buk!*'

'What?'

'You nearly gave me a cardiac arrest, *that's what?* How did you get in?'

Buk looked momentarily mystified. He blinked, his white lashes catching the sunlight.

'The door, of course.' Nancy propped herself up in her bed, feeling a dull ache in her left arm.

'Gosh, you're hilarious. OK, then ... *why* are you here?'

'I've got something to show you!' he announced. He held up the Codice. 'It's working again! I don't know how long for, we may not have much time ... '

'We ....?' Nancy narrowed her eyes dangerously, but Buk seemed to be completely immune to nuance.

'Yes – you and me.' He turned one of his solemn looks on her. 'I've been thinking about what you said. I can still help you, if you want.'

Nancy began to feel angry all over again.

'I don't want anyone's help. Why do you all think I'm a charity case?'

'This could be your last chance.'

'My last chance for what?'

'To understand.'

Nancy flung herself back on her bed. 'What if I don't want any explanations, what if I can't be bothered?'

Buk should have looked exasperated at this point, but he didn't. 'You said yourself,' he just sounded patient, 'you wish things to be simple.' Nancy did a quick rewind of her conversations.

'I never said that, I just thought it.'

'The Codice might not work again.'

'So?'

'Nancy, it's not just your story, it's everyone's – we're all in this thing together. This is what you humans forget sometimes.'

Nancy, who had pulled the cover over her head, slowly drew it back to look at him. She had suspected all along that he might not be completely human but hearing it from him felt important. She looked at him for a long while and he stared calmly back. She had to admit she had missed Buk in the last few days and she was glad enough to see him not to be angry anymore. Glad to see he looked thin but happy. It was pretty tragic, but Buk was probably her only friend these days.

'OK,' she said eventually, 'let's get it over with.'

This time he handed her the Codice.

As she took it, Nancy felt something delicate beat under its warm surface, like a pulse of a small animal. It was comforting in her hands, as if this living thing could heal by touch alone. Experimentally, she ran her fingers over the surface and noticed how the symbols came alive under her fingers in the same way it worked for Buk. She felt flattered, as if it had started to recognise her.

Stroking her fingertips across the jumble of runes, symbols and letters she heard snatches of whispered words and phrases.

'You still haven't told me how it works,' she remarked, surprising herself with a realisation: Buk and his Codice were the same thing: neither fully of the world but some kind of bridge, maybe?

Nancy was drawn in enough to believe that much.

Buk, who was standing very close to her, his cheek almost resting against hers, paused before answering. 'The Codice is Legend.'

Nancy raised an eyebrow. 'That's not exactly helpful, is it?'

Buk frowned as if steeling himself to make an effort for her sake. 'Each one of us, even me, carries with us the imprint of our genes, of the generations of own species and the species that came before us, and before them. These are our *other memories* – the parts of us that are only us through our common inheritance. The Codice could show you star systems light years away because this is where we all come from – particles and molecules that travelled through space for billions of years, eventually coming to rest here on this Earth and forming life. Every molecule in our body was once in the heart of our Sun. Our star.'

'Oh,' said Nancy, noticing that each time Buk spoke the Codice got warmer, evidently reacting to his voice.

'Our *other memories* tell us to seek out the light and to fear the dark. They teach us to distinguish good from bad, beauty from ugliness, hope from despair, when despair seems the only logical response ... '. He paused again. 'So what do you see?' he prompted. Nancy looked long and hard at the Codice. She saw her mother's concerned face and light falling across sheets... *not yet,* a voice whispered in her head, *but soon.* Nancy concentrated and something else came into focus.

'I see a library.'

'That sounds like a good place to start.'

Chapter 17

Leather-bound books lined the walls and a grand-father clock in an alcove went *tick, and* then *tock,* with some authority.

At the far end of the room, a set of French windows, standing half open, led onto a stone veranda that looked out over an English rose garden in full bloom.

Nancy stepped carefully past the shelves stacked high with volumes whose titles were picked out in gold leaf and vermillion dye and stopped about four feet away from the girl with blond hair in a sky blue dress. The young lady, who must have been a year or two older than Nancy, looked up and smiled openly. She was reading a book with a large rabbit on the front cover.

'Where am I?' asked Nancy.

The girl stood up and took Nancy's hand in hers.

'You are where you have always been.'

'Where's that?'

'You'll find out, you just need to be patient,' she said. 'Would you like some tea? I can ring for cake, it's usually something grown-up like ginger and fig but sometimes they make a sponge … ?' Nancy let go of the girl's hand and walked past her to the open French windows. She looked for a moment at the roses and an ornamental fountain shaped like a top hat.

'Um … no thanks … ,' she paused as if something had suddenly occurred to her. 'I *can* leave here if I want to?'

'Yes, of course you can. You can go anywhere you want now.'

'I can?'

'Just look for a door.'

'Like … ' Nancy pointed out into the garden, 'that one?'

Her companion laughed.

'That's a bit obvious, isn't it?'

'Oh.' Nancy cast around. In the corner, by a large brass lamp with a green shade, there was a picture. Nancy could make very little out, except for a sense of swirling clouds and what looked like the tip of a wing. On instinct she pointed at the etching.

The girl in the blue dress with pale eyes studied Nancy for a long moment. 'Buk said you were clever … yes, that is a simply perfect choice.'

Before she could think of a reply, Nancy was falling in a maelstrom of noise, lashing rain and winds stronger than she imagined were possible. Her first instinct was to wrap herself up tightly into a ball but, when she did so, she had a terrifying sense of going into freefall. So she flayed in panic and felt her descent halt abruptly.

Nancy looked across and noticed that her arms were now huge, leathery wings that extended several metres in either direction; strong membranes that linked the joints and sinews beat the air as she banked, punching a hole the size of a house through the black twisting cloud of a cyclone.

Just a minute, it was coming back to her now.

She was *StormDriver* – the most powerful, stately and, generally-considered, vainest dragon to have ruled the stratosphere.

This was what she just wanted – no, needed: power and freedom.

She opened her mouth to laugh and a majestic jet of white-hot flames exploded into the air, searing a tunnel through the wind and the rain, momentarily taming the eye of the storm itself.

Enough!

She lashed her tail and straightened her neck, going into a dive like an eight-ton missile of taught sinew, flesh, fire and vengeance. As she came out of the cloud she realised, with a brief jolt of vertigo, that she was well over a mile up – the landscape below her was densely wooded but for a lake, which reflected what little light there was on its troubled surface. Another door!

She flattened her wings against her body and sharpened her trajectory; hurtling, seconds later, into the freezing water.

There was a short, sharp shock as ice enveloped her great jaws and head.

… and then suddenly Nancy was back – more or less as herself – in broad daylight, standing at the top of a tall round tower surrounded by undulating valleys and thick forest.

The trees surrounding the base of the tower had been cleared to within fifty or so yards of the walls and it stood silent in deep snow that glowed pinkish white in the pale winter sun.

In this new fairytale, Nancy's hair now hung in long, golden tresses and she wore a gown in red velvet, trimmed with white fur. She was the eternal princess, trapped in a tower, or perhaps protected in it: because, actually, she felt perfectly cosy and safe as she stared out across the ice-bound landscape, beyond the trees to a distant road that led far beyond the horizon.

Each day she woke at dawn to find warm bread, some meat and a bowl of perfectly ripe fruit on a wooden table by the fire. A pewter jug contained water; and a crystal decanter, sweet wine.

There was no doorway leading out of the room and she did vaguely wonder who provided the food each day.

After breakfast, Nancy would go onto the balcony and look out at the view – usually at the winding road that led away to somewhere other than the deserted wood but sometimes, just for a change, she described a half-circle of the tower and stared (as if mesmerised) at the dark wall of trees, trying to make out what lay in the shadows under the sloping boughs.

One day, just as she was about to retire for the evening, she spotted a lone figure approaching the tower along the road. It was hard to tell how far off the figure was in the twilight, so she went to bed without thinking much more about the matter. She was learning that letting things come, in their own time, was often the best answer.

The next morning the figure turned out to be a small man on a large white horse, about four hundred yards away. He must have stopped during the night, but he was now galloping towards the tower at great speed, as if he'd left his wallet inside with strangers.

Nancy, who had seen not a soul for weeks, felt suddenly rather afraid, so she ducked back from the balustrade and hid behind her bed, which – apart from the wooden table – was the only other furniture in the room.

A few minutes later a sharp, somewhat hectoring voice drifted up to where Nancy crouched.

'Fairness, I am here, your Prince Charming! I have come to rescue you. Tell me the magic word and I will deliver you from this enchanted place. You may come and live with me in my castle and I will make you one of my seven brides!'

Not on your nelly, thought Nancy and she made loud snoring sounds as if she was fast asleep.

Things got annoying after that. Each day the man came and repeated his proposal. Sometimes he also offered her gold and bits of gaudy jewellery.

He would strut up and down, under the miniature battlements, like a peacock, rubbing his hands together, spitting into the snow. Nancy, peeking down from above grimaced, noticing that he was, in fact, not human at all but some sort of squat gargoyle. He had lumpy, misshapen features – tinged grey-ish green – and a protruding lower jaw. He also had a bald patch flecked with dandruff when he took off his helmet.

Nancy started to look seriously for a hidden door.

Then one day she got up and noticed that the horrible little troglodyte had gone. She wondered if he'd given up. However, a day or so later, he came back with a large axe and a look of grim determination on his ugly face.

Before she had time to shout anything out he started to hammer at the tower's walls. The stonework turned out to be surprisingly poor and within minutes the whole building began to shake and then sway. She had to think fast. Dashing into the room she looked this way and that and her eye alighted on the crystal decanter full of wine. She ran, as fast as she could, back to the balcony.

'Sto ... *desist* fair Prince!' she shouted, 'verily, by your fortitude and perseverance, you have shown yourself worthy of my hand. Lay down your axe and remove your helmet, so I can gaze with love upon your fine face!'

The small monster didn't need asking twice. With impatient fingers he loosened the chinstraps and tore off his helmet.

The action was perfectly timed with the crystal wine decanter, which hit him square on his bald patch.

It burst with a satisfying sound of breaking glass and he went down with a short grunt of surprise.

The minute the liquid hit the snow, creepers grew up, over his unconscious body, latching onto the walls of the tower, and quickly reaching the balcony. Nancy grabbed some bread and climbed down as best she could, jumping the last few feet into the thick snow.

Instinctively avoiding the road, she ran towards the dark forest. As she came closer she was able to see that her instinct was right – something lay in the shaded area under the trees. It looked like a small bundle of rags, lying immobile in the snow, and she ran towards it.

Gasping for breath in the cold air, cursing her long dress that made running almost bloody impossible, she got to the figure and crouched down beside him and the small stone that was nearby.

Buk's face was blue with cold and he was barely breathing.

Suddenly she understood that Buk was the door, all along. Nancy finally realised she was in complete control. She blinked and murmured, 'Home', and, before she knew it, she was back on her bed, sitting cross-legged, watching the sun come up over the trees.

Chapter 18

Buk was in trouble, she knew that. However, despite searching frantically all day, she didn't find him until late evening.

Nancy revisited Falaise Square at least six times as she criss-crossed the Marketplace, ducking down the side streets and walkways that made a human rabbit warren out of the old part of town. She even went along the river, almost all the way to Marsh Lock, past the museum – noticing how the children, students, and tourists all seemed to have got sick of ice cream and walked about, instead, with great bottles of frosted tap water.

By now, she was pretty sure that the Earth wasn't slowing down and that the heatwave was probably only temporary but that wasn't the point: Buk believed it and his conviction was killing the Codice and possibly even him. She had heard of people dying from a broken heart before and Nancy guessed that this wasn't much different.

She tried the library, the college and even the church at the far end of town by the bridge; feeling increasingly panicky as ghostly images of his frozen face that she had seen in the enchanted forest appeared at random in car windows and shop fronts.

His intrusion into the fairytale of the Forest and Tower was a message – a sort of cry for help. Stories and what was real were no different for him, he could slip between the two and that had been his gift to Nancy. But why? She still didn't know the answer to that, but the fact that real life and fairy tale seemed to be merging felt like they were creeping towards a conclusion. Perhaps this strange sense of unreality would fall away from Nancy, like a dark veil and her head would clear. Then she might be able to help Buk, like he was trying to help her.

That's what friends did.

At about six o'clock she had begun yet another circuit of the town, this time walking and then jogging in short agitated bursts of nervous energy. *Where was he, where was he, where was he …?* – her breath, by now, was coming in short hiccupy gasps – he was very ill, even dying somewhere … but where …?

Quite suddenly, she had a brainwave.

When she got to the cemetery it wasn't immediately obvious where he was, but she felt his ebbing, pale presence, here, amongst the stones, the dry grass and wilted flowers.

When she found him, just as the sun was starting to dip below the line of pine trees that circled the cemetery, he was lying between some large grey bins and a pile of leaves left over from winter. She had to force herself not to cry as she picked him up, amazed and heartbroken at his lightness. He was somehow shrunken now, like a very small boy. Like her baby brother in a few years ... if he lived.

If.

'I'm sorry Buk,' she said. 'It's all my fault, I let you get like this. If I had believed you sooner and not thought I was going mad and blamed you ... I could have helped you.'

His eyes fluttered and he smiled. 'You found me.'

~

Stumbling out of the gates she ran up to a group of men in suits, their collars undone, talking loudly on their way home. 'Help!' she half-shouted. 'My friend needs help ... ' but the men just fell silent, their faces turning from jocular to stony indifference as they stepped around her and moved on up the road.

A couple of cars came into view, picking up speed at the start of the Fairmile in order to make the ascent of the sharp hill that led out of town towards Oxford. She missed the first but tried to wave the second one down by flapping her free arm and stepping boldly into the road. It nearly hit her, and Nancy jumped back, almost dropping Buk as she felt the wind from the car buffet her, its wing mirror missing her elbow by millimetres.

At this rate she was going to get them both killed.

There was only one thing for it – she would have to take Buk to her house. It was too early for her father to be back but she could phone for an ambulance and her mother would know what to do.

Buk murmured something and stirred in her arms as she stumbled along, half running. The Codice, which had been safely stowed in his tunic up until now, slipped and Nancy had to stop to push it back. She was shocked when she touched it – the surface was as stiff and lifeless as old cardboard.

Nancy was wondering what this meant and so she hardly noticed the ambulance that sped past her, turning, with an audible screech of tyres, onto the main road that led away from their house. However, it was followed closely by her father's old blue Volvo, which she saw all too clearly, with a start – its boot door swinging open as it came past. Her father was alone in the front, his hands gripping the steering wheel, his eyes staring blindly ahead.

The car had to slow when it reached Nancy since the ambulance in front had just stopped before making the second turning that took it onto the main Oxford road. On impulse Nancy jumped clumsily into the open boot with Buk still in her arms. She was just about to say something when the boot door swung shut just as her dad pulled away with a jolt. Its heavy lid must have hit her on the back of the head because she slumped forwards, unconscious.

It seemed like hours later that she came to in the hospital car park, still in the boot of the car. The sky was dark and it was much colder. She peered over the row of back seats. The clock on the dashboard told her that it was 20:47. Buk was lying half underneath her and her head ached worse than usual.

Thanking her luck that the central locking on the old car hadn't worked properly for years, she let herself out and pulled Buk gently towards the lip of the boot.

As she was about to lift him again he opened his eyes. 'Nancy,' he said and smiled wanly.

She slid her forearms under his body but he pushed her away gently. 'I can walk,' he said. 'Are we at the hospital?'

Nancy nodded.

'Yes. I think my mother was rushed here just after I found you. I have to get you inside and then I've got to find her.' She did her best to sound calm but, even so, her voice sounded shaky and odd to her ears. Buk got up and moved slowly but determinedly towards the slipway which led up to the main doors.

'Then you must follow me, I'll lead the way it doesn't matter about me,' he said over his shoulder.

Nancy had started to feel the identical sense of barely concealed panic she had experienced when she was last here. Not now she thought, *not this time,* but it was a few moments before she could pluck up the courage to follow Buk and, when she did, she realised that he had already disappeared inside.

The sight of the hospital doors sent a surge of fear through her whole body, making her feel like curling herself into a tight ball. But she kept going, moving as fast as she could up the ramp, giving herself mom- entum as she ran towards the revolving doors. She felt shaky and vaguely aware of the slap of a crisp wrapper that had got stuck between the rubber matting and door jamb, as she stumbled into the brightly lit reception area that smelled of instant coffee, antiseptic and anxiety.

She looked around wildly for Buk, knowing that if she didn't see him soon then she would most likely turn around there and then and flee in blind terror, away from the hospital.

But she caught sight of his retreating silhouette down a long, polished corridor that led off to quite another part of the hospital. Nancy was fairly certain that maternity was on the first floor in this block and that her mother would be there but she didn't trust herself to go alone, so she ran after Buk, surprised and curious that he seemed to have recovered enough to walk.

Nancy got to the end of the corridor just in time to see his bare foot slip around the corner of another ward where a brightly coloured mural of a pre-historic jungle scene took up a whole section of wall.

'Buk, wait!' she shouted but he had already disappeared. She ran after him before the door clicked shut and so slipped unnoticed into what must have been the children's ward. It should have felt better in here, with the soft-play mats in reception, the neatly arranged picture books, colouring pens and the dimmed lighting that suggested the ward had already shut for the night.

But it felt a lot worse and Nancy experienced a tightening in her stomach that almost brought her to her knees. She had the feeling that something was waiting for her here, in this ward – almost as if it were luring her in.

'Here, Nancy.'

Buk stood at the far end of the corridor, beckoning her. She turned towards him, trying to ignore her headache that made her skull pound like it was about to split in two like an over-ripe melon. Buk slipped into a private room whose door lay half-open, a blue light spilling out into the dim corridor.

She drew a deep breath and, summoning up the very last reserves of her courage, she followed him in.

Chapter 19

❦

Nancy stood at the foot of the bed looking at *herself* lying there, so pale that she was almost lost against the white sheets. Tears ran freely down her face. They fell onto her hands that clenched and unclenched the clean linen. This confused her – if she was just a ghost, then why did the tears seem real?

'I don't understand,' she said. But she did – the headaches, the sense of being apart the last few weeks – it suddenly all made sense. 'How long have I been here?' she asked with a huge effort to control her voice. Buk raised his eyes from where he had been studying the wasted body of the real Nancy that was lying in the bed, a tube taped to the side of her mouth and another leading to her stomach. One side of her head was swathed in bandages, the other covered with a marble-work of fading bruises.

'They took you here after the car crash a few weeks ago. You've been unconscious ever since.'

'And,' Nancy moved her arm in a short arc, beginning to feel almost angry, 'what about all this?' Buk looked puzzled.

'What?'

' ... what's been happening to my mother and the baby ... '

'Nancy,' said Buk coming over to her unsteadily, 'your mother was driving ... she blames herself, she also thinks she's going to lose you. Your father is trying his best to give her hope. And she nearly lost the baby ... she may yet ... I'm so sorry.' Nancy swallowed, forcing herself to look at her own body lying there, to come to terms with it.

' ... and what about the stories, the Codice, the heat ... you?'

Buk parted his lips with the faintest of *puh* sounds. 'they gave you time ... '

'For what?'

'So you could make the right decision.'

Nancy shook her head. 'I still don't understand – what decision do I have to make?'

'Stay,' said Buk simply, gesturing at her broken body, 'or go.' He let his hand drop.

'Go back to the stories?'

'Yes, you could go back there, or ... somewhere else.' Buk trailed off, seemingly unsure how to finish.

Nancy stood there considering herself. She thought of the dragon, its power, *her* power and the feeling of safety and peace in the tower before the stunted monster turned up. Nancy remembered the linnet singing in the frosty air, and the uncomplicated joy of the children playing in the garden. She thought it was going to be an easy decision – stories were comforting, they made sense. But then she saw something in the corner of the room on the back of a plastic chair.

It was a dark green cardigan her mother often wore. On impulse, she went over to the table and picked it up. Bringing the soft wool up to her tear-stained face, she closed her eyes and inhaled.

When she opened them she had decided. She nodded at Buk and he brushed the hair from her eyes.

Chapter 20

A long time after, Nancy heard squeaky footsteps in her room and opened one eye a
fraction.

She was lying in her hospital, back, alive! *Really*
alive. A wave of relief and happiness flooded through
her, making the newly-experienced pain in her head
and arm seem insignificant. In fact, better than
insignificant – the pain felt real, and somehow so
much better than the half life she had been living out
of her body for the past few weeks. She had made the
right decision. A woman doctor was standing at the
foot of her bed, studying her chart. She looked up as a
nurse entered the room in a sort of controlled hurry.

'Doctor?' the nurse sounded Australian.

'Oh, hi Mo', the doctor's voice was light and casual,
and Nancy had a fleeting impression that these two
may also be friends as well as work colleagues. 'Take
a look at this.' The nurse looked at the chart and then
shot a glance at the monitor by Nancy's head. She
looked puzzled.

'It's um, amazing ... you don't think there's been a mistake?'

'No, I double-checked it but that's why I called you in, I wanted a second opinion before rounds start in the morning – you know what Mr. Webb is like.'

'Point taken.' On second thoughts the doctor sounded Australian too – perhaps that's why they were friendly; but Nancy wasn't good with accents – she once asked a girl from Wales at her school if she thought Edinburgh was a bit touristy. The nurse tapped the clipboard she was holding with the end of her pen and continued. 'Well all her vitals have stabilised and so I'd say she was safely out of the coma. It's incredible, even a day ago, I wouldn't have given her more than a one in twenty chance of pulling through, especially with a head injury like that. Kids – you never can tell – they're often stronger than they look.' Her doctor friend smiled somewhat tiredly then stretched.

'Hmm, another miracle at the John Radcliffe – one for the staff newsletter. I'll give you the pleasure of telling the parents.'

'Thanks Shona. We've all been upset about this one. I heard that the driver in the other car fell asleep at the wheel – he was sentenced yesterday, suspended for three years. It would have been five but he had a clean record and a family too – he's devastated, to be fair, admitted guilt, short trial … you know.' By way of a response the doctor nodded noncommittally, as if the legal system was not her concern.

'Goodnight Mo, see you in rounds in three hours – I'm going to try and get some shut-eye.'

Nancy waited for a few moments, making sure they had gone but she must have been trying too hard to pretend to be asleep because she actually dropped off. For the first time in weeks, she slipped into a proper sleep. No dreams this time, just peaceful, blissful rest.

When she awoke, the room was empty and the tube had been removed from her mouth. Her jaw ached and she felt a bit light-headed but that was all. Pale grey light filtered in through the gaps in the blinds and Nancy guessed that it must have been very early in the morning, just before dawn.

She lay there quietly for a while and then, when she was sure that no-one was about, she slipped from her bed, allowing the tips of her bare toes to rest on the cold, turquoise linoleum for a few moments before trusting her legs to take her full weight.

Even so, when she did try to stand, her knees immediately buckled and Nancy had to grab the sheet to stop herself from falling over. Leaning across the cool bed linen, she rested for a few moments, allowing her head to clear, testing her weight on each foot. When she was sure she felt strong enough, she pushed away from the bed and tottered towards the door.

The corridor outside was cool and quiet as she walked past a large aquarium full of darting, silver fish. Here and there, children stirred in their beds as she padded by, shakily re-tracing her steps from earlier, back through the ward and into the main part of the hospital. There was no sign of Buk but she felt no fear, just a new-found confidence inside, in the hospital. In the reception area there was a sudden flurry of activity as she came around the corner. A very tall old man in a brown dressing gown and muffler was refusing to put his cigarette out and two members of staff were arguing with him whilst everyone else looked on.

He stopped shouting and stared at Nancy intently whilst a member of the reception staff tried to prise the stub of his cigarette out of his huge fingers.

Nancy passed by unnoticed by everyone else and slipped down the corridor marked *Maternity*.

Her mother's room was almost exactly the same as hers, only slightly larger. More tubes, two monitors and a steady *pip/beep* noise coming from somewhere that meant nothing to Nancy but somehow sounded reassuring. In the corner her father, looking rumpled and unshaved, slept soundly in a chair and, next to him, a clear plastic tub on wheels housed a small mound of blue blankets.

Nancy approached her mother's bed just as she opened her eyes. They stared at one another.

'My darling, my beautiful girl,' her mother whispered. 'I dreamt of you – you were alone.' A small tear escaped the corner of her eye and blossomed on the clean white sheet. 'I felt you so many times, these past few weeks … is it really you?'

In answer, Nancy lent over the bed and held onto her mother for a very, very long time.

A while later, a shuffling sound caught her attention and she looked up as Buk came in. Both her parents slept and his quiet entrance had not made them stir. So pale now, he could have been a spectre himself –

he tried to smile but staggered forward and nearly fell. Nancy knew that she wouldn't have the strength to carry him but she didn't need to. how she could help him.

She tiptoed across the room and gently lifted the tiny bundle that lay in the cot.

'Buk … you think the world is ending and I may not be as old or as clever as you, but I do know that your worst enemy cannot harm you as much as your own thoughts. You taught me to love what I have.

'You also told me there are no stories left but this is my baby brother – he's brand new and he is perfect. He has his whole life ahead of him – one long fantastic story that is his to share. And so do I, thanks to you.' And so she brought the baby's head up level with Buk's as he lay there, barely breathing.

He didn't stir for a few moments and at first she thought she was too late.

Then his chest heaved and Buk's eyelids fluttered open. He stared at the sleeping baby for what seemed like an age and Nancy saw something change in his face. She wouldn't have known how to describe *hope* before that morning but now she had a pretty good idea. Perfectly on cue, a small hand reached out from the soft blankets and gripped one of Buk's slender fingers.

And then, just at that moment, the sun cleared the trees and shone into the room, heralding a new day, and Buk simply disappeared in its glare.

Epilogue

N ancy was pretty sure she would never see Buk again and she would have been right had she not, in her ninety-eighth year, chanced to look into the reflection of a shop window when she was feeling giddy.

It was a glorious day and the papers were already talking about the hottest summer since records began. Not as hot as 1990 some said, when Nancy was caught between childhood and being grown up, but that was so long ago and Nancy had learned to take newspaper statistics with a pinch of salt.

Her youngest granddaughter had a birthday coming up and she had taken her to town to buy her something to wear that she liked but was probably going to be dreadful. It *was* hot and Nancy had forgotten her pills. It was hardly surprising then, that when she stood up quickly (they had stopped for sorbets at a small outdoor café in New Hart Street), she felt suddenly very light-headed and had to sit down again with a bump – as if playing a party game.

'Are you alright granny?' her granddaughter had just taken her arm and was vaguely looking around for a proper adult to take charge. Nancy didn't hear her at first, or at least didn't answer – she was smiling, apparently into thin air, at something across the street.

On a stone, in the corner of the cobbled square, sat a barefoot boy with white-blond hair and a look that she remembered from nearly a century before. He smiled back at her and waved.

MONSTER BOOKS

Henley-on-Thames . MMXXI

The Hairy Hand

When **Septimus** inherits a magical, treasure-finding **Hairy Hand** from his uncle, life suddenly becomes a lot more exciting – **and dangerous!**

A scary adventure for 8 -12 year olds, full of jokes, magical familiars and a Dickensian cast.

For details of where to buy this and other titles, just go to

www.monsterbooks.co.uk

The Angel Of Mons

Ben's father is in prison and his mum, a former child genius, is barely hanging on to her sanity. When Ben and his classmates are nearly killed in a coach crash in Belgium, Ben starts to experience flashbacks: visitations to the brutal start of **World War 1** and the uncertain world of **Corporal Sam Lyle**. Is Ben going mad, or is there another reason why he finds himself in a war zone in 1914? Who is the spectral figure that haunts both the boy and the soldier? **Do angels exist?**

For details of where to buy this and other titles, just go to

www.monsterbooks.co.uk

Small Vampires

Out October 2021 • 10th Anniversary edition

Turn your gaze to a half-remembered world of childhood that exists below the tall grass and flowering hedgerows. Look very carefully and you may be able to trace the remains of minute pathways through the undergrowth, leading to small mounds of dry foliage in curious, deliberate shapes – Leaf Castles! These are perhaps the last visible remains of the Hidden Kingdom.

A **mysterious volume** in an **unknown tongue**, a thief who could change the course of the world, and a closely guarded secret **older than Humankind**.

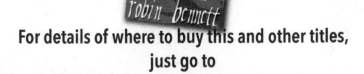

For details of where to buy this and other titles, just go to

www.monsterbooks.co.uk